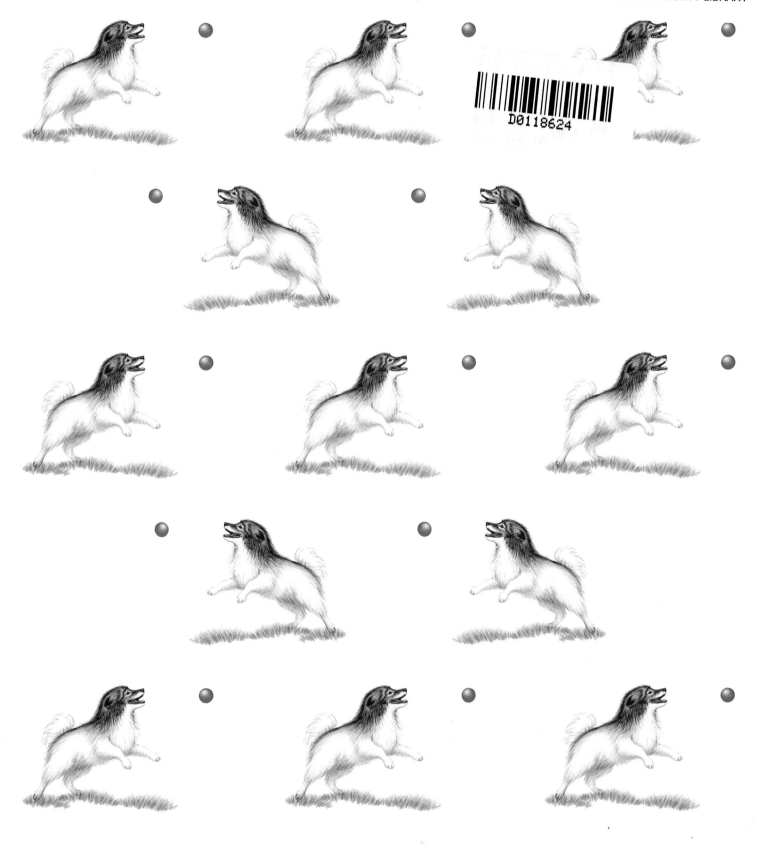

The Gryphon Press

—a voice for the voiceless—

This book is dedicated, with sincere gratitude,
to each person who rescues, fosters, adopts, and takes responsible care of an animal.

To those who have struggled through illness and abuse into a world of love and hope.
—Jan Zita Grover

To all people who welcome abandoned pets into their lives and hearts.
—Nancy Lane

A portion of profits from this book will be donated to
humane education programs, to shelters, and to animal rescue societies.

Sit! Stay! Read! Series

Copyright © 2008 text by Jan Zita Grover
Copyright © 2008 art by Nancy Lane
All rights reserved. This book, or parts thereof,
may not be reproduced without permission from the publisher,
The Gryphon Press, 6808 Margaret's Lane, Edina, MN 55439.

Reg. U.S. Patent. & Tm Office. The scanning, uploading and distribution
of this book via the Internet or via any other means without the permission
of the publisher is illegal and punishable by law. Please purchase only authorized
electronic editions, and do not participate in or encourage electronic piracy of copyrighted
materials. Your support of the author's and artist's rights is appreciated.

Text design by Connie Kuhnz
Text set in Galliard by Prism Publishing Center
Manufactured in Canada by Friesens Corporation

Library of Congress Control Number: 2007936274

ISBN: 978-0-940719-05-7

1 3 5 7 9 10 8 6 4 2

I am the voice of the voiceless:
Through me, the dumb shall speak;
Till the deaf world's ear be made to hear
The cry of the wordless weak.

—from a poem by Ella Wheeler Wilcox, early 20th-century poet

A Home for Dakota

Jan Zita Grover   •   Nancy Lane

In that place,
it was always dark and cold.

We lived in shaky towers of wire crates,
dogs above and dogs below. We could hear each other,
but we couldn't touch or see or warm each other.

It was cold,
and I had no fur.

The only warmth I remember was
puppies—many, many puppies. But they were
taken away each time, and I didn't see them again.

One chilly morning, lights crisscrossed our darkness.
The big doors swung open, and I saw the lighted eyes of trucks.

Our towers of cages came down. A human they called Emma
with a low, comforting voice carried my crate
into the inside of a truck.

I fell asleep in the unfamiliar rocking warmth.

One chilly morning, lights crisscrossed our darkness.
The big doors swung open, and I saw the lighted eyes of trucks.

Our towers of cages came down. A human they called Emma
with a low, comforting voice carried my crate
into the inside of a truck.

I fell asleep in the unfamiliar rocking warmth.

I awoke in a soft nest. Beyond me I saw very bright light.
I could see fresh water in a corner of my little room.
I hadn't walked for so long that I could hardly take a step
without falling.

"You can do it, sweet girl! You can do it!"
cried Emma.

My feet were sore.
My long nails slipped
and slid on the shiny floor.

I fell down hard and couldn't get up again.
My insides melted, and hot pee flowed out of me. I began to pant.
I just wanted to go back into the familiar dark.

"There, there, little sister," Emma said.
"I'm going to give you a new name.
You aren't just number 241 anymore—you're Dakota now."

"I'm going to clean you up, and you'll feel better."

"The fur on the tips of your ears can grow back now."

"I think your coat will grow back, too."

"You won't itch anymore."

"This ointment should take care of your eye infection."

I wanted to thank her. I licked her hand.

"Thank you, Dakota," she said,
and she hugged me.

It was my first hug.

Emma carried me back to my warm nest in a big towel.
Waiting for me was a bowl of wonderful-smelling food.
My mouth flooded from sudden hunger.

I ate and ate, and then I settled down and slept again.

Days followed days, and sometimes I walked painfully
down the hall to visit Emma in her office.
While she worked, I lay at her feet, listening to the rustle
of her papers until I slept.

I started to grow wisps of fur.

"You're almost ready now, sweet Dakota," Emma would say. "Look at you—you look like a little dandelion."

One morning Emma brought three other people to see me.
The small one didn't have any more fur on her head than I did.

"I don't like her—she's ugly!" the girl said.
"She doesn't have any fur, and her ears are all
weird—they look like they've been chewed.
And look—someone cut her tail!"

I didn't understand many human words yet,
but I knew when words were kind or mean.
These sounded mean.

I began to shake all over.

"Dakota is growing new hair, Sweetie," Emma said, "just like you will when you get better. Wouldn't it be fun to grow new hair together?"

"No," the girl named Sweetie said. "I want a *perfect* dog."

Emma came back to see me after they left.

"Don't feel bad, Dakota," she said. "I've been out to visit them, and I think they're the right family for you. Sweetie's going to love you for who you are. She just needs a little time."

Many days later, those three came back.
Sweetie looked at me again,
and this time her voice sounded kind.

"I've been thinking a lot about you, Dakota," she said.
"Let's try."

I didn't want to leave Emma
and the dear familiar smells and sounds.

"Just try it, little Dakota," Emma said.
"I'll be waiting for you if it doesn't work out."

I rode away in a warm car alongside Sweetie.

"I can practically count your hairs," she said and laughed. "Mine, too."

Sweetie has a big nest, and I get to sleep in it.
I curl up with her when she isn't feeling well,
and when she reads, and when she sleeps.

Sometimes Sweetie rubs good-smelling stuff all over my feet
because Emma told her it would heal them.

Sweetie says, "I'm so sorry, Dakota.
I'm sorry for every day I didn't take you home."

I don't count days the way people do.
Sweetie loves me, and I love her.

That's all that matters.

And we've both been growing hair.

Helping Dogs Like Dakota (for parents and other adults)

What Is a Puppy Mill? Puppy mills are wholesale dog stockbreeding operations. Most puppy mill dogs are bred from weak, sick, unsocialized dams and sires; they are prone to ill health and genetic problems. Puppies receive little human attention and are often left unwormed and unprotected against disease. Most of these dogs are sold to pet stores.

Conditions: Puppy mill breed stock typically live in wire crates, some of them stacked five to seven high; the urine and feces from dogs above fall on the dogs below. Long-tailed dogs may have their tails removed so that they fit into smaller crates. Dogs lose their coats to malnutrition, mange, and other infections. Because the dogs are not exercised and stand in crates too small for them to move about, their toenails grow so long that they cannot walk when removed from their prisons. When the demand for a breed's pups goes down, or a breeding dog no longer has puppies, the dogs are abandoned, killed, sold off to another puppy mill, or dumped at a shelter.

How Can We Get Rid of Puppy Mills?
Legislation that prohibits these large breeding operations is the long-term solution. At this time, a patchwork of laws is supposed to protect dogs in puppy mills, but the resources for good enforcement simply aren't there, and dogs continue to suffer every day, even in mills that have been found repeatedly to be in violation of existing laws. Most puppy mill operators who are raided and shut down are those reported by neighbors, members of breed rescue groups, or people from local shelters.

What Can You Do? Don't buy dogs from anyone whose home or business you have not personally visited. If you do not buy companion animals from a pet shop or on the Internet, you will help wipe out the financial reward for breeders, and puppy mills will close for lack of business. Millions of unwanted dogs (many purebreds) die every year in shelters for lack of a home. Adopt a dog from your local shelter. If you want a specific breed of dog, seek out a breed rescue group—there's one for every kind of dog out there.

Puppy Mill Dogs as Companion Animals: These dogs' chief experience of human beings is as wielders of force, not as kind and steady presences. Puppy mill rescue dogs, whether pups or adult "breeding stock," need regular routines and a quiet home in which to recover from their ordeals. Most rescue groups do not adopt out puppy mill rescues until they have first spent months learning to live in family homes. Like all dogs, puppy mill rescue dogs are individuals and vary in their ability to recover from abuse: some can become excellent family companions, while others need the quiet predictability of homes with adults.

Resources: The following organizations (listed alphabetically) have Web sites that offer additional information. ***Warning:*** *the videos and photographs on some of the sites show brutal and distressing conditions.* <u>*Young children should not view them.*</u>

American Society for the Prevention of Cruelty to Animals
http://www.aspca.org/site/PageServer?pagename=cruelty_puppymills

The Humane Society of the United States
http://www.stoppuppymills.org

Prisoners of Greed, Coalition Against Misery
http://www.prisonersofgreed.org/Commercial-kennel-facts.html

Puppymill Rescue
http://www.puppymillrescue.com/

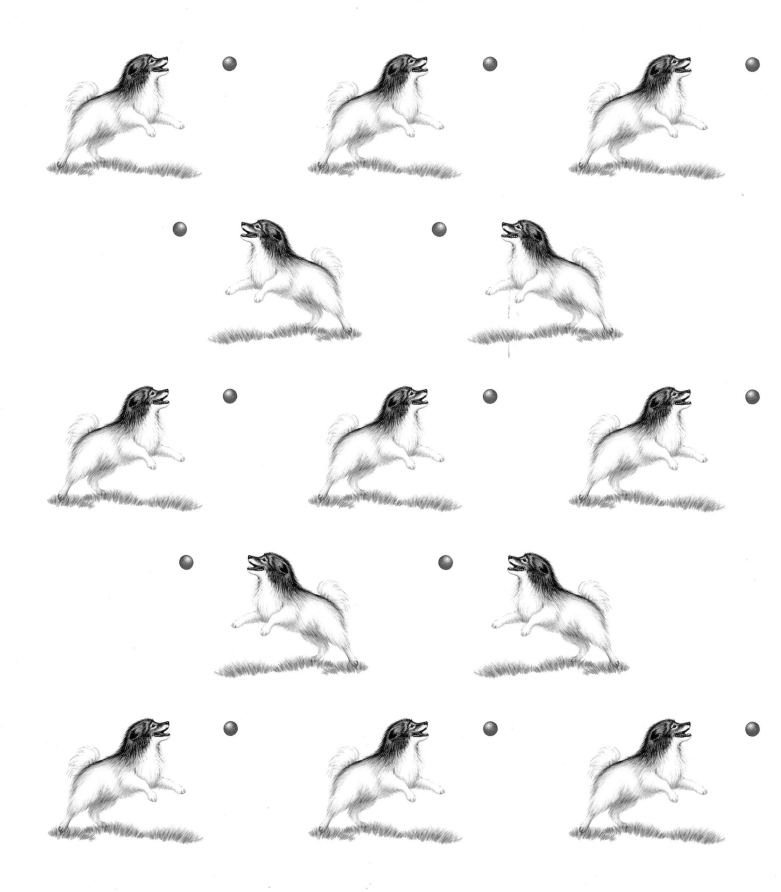